To: Mackenzie & Spencer

From: Nate & Haley

Santa's Hawaiian Holiday

written by **Malia Collins** • illustrated by **Linda Maliuana Oszajca**

BEACHHOUSE

For Max and Mehana—MC

For Kamalei, Hoʻokahua, Lokelani, Hoʻolana, Makamae
and my future moʻopuna—LO

Library of Congress Cataloging-in-Publication Data
Collins, Malia.
Santa's Hawaiian holiday / written by Malia Collins ; illustrated by Linda Oszajca.
p. cm.
Summary: While vacationing in beautiful Hawaii, Santa Claus neglects his duties at the North Pole.
ISBN-13: 978-1-933067-21-6
ISBN-10: 1-933067-21-7 (hardcover : alk. paper)
[1. Hawaii--Fiction. 2. Santa Claus--Fiction.] I. Oszajca, Linda, ill. II. Title.
PZ7.C69665San 2007
[E]--dc22
2007025762
ISBN-10: 1-933067-21-7
ISBN-13: 978-1-933067-21-6

First Printing, October 2007
Second Printing, September 2009

BeachHouse Publishing, LLC
PO Box 5464
Kāneʻohe, Hawaiʻi 96744
email: info@beachhousepublishing.com
www.beachhousepublishing.com
Printed in Korea

NorthPole Times

Breaking News!

December 1st
North Pole—Breaking News!—Santa Reported Missing

Last night, suddenly bright lights were seen flying across the sky. Reindeer were missing from their stalls. And a workshop full of confused elves was in a small panic. When asked of Santa's whereabouts, a seemingly calm Mrs. Claus replied, "No Comment."

I was tired. I was beat. I needed a rest.

Even Mrs. Claus said, "Nick, you're not looking your best."
Such a cold, snowy place, that's my home, The North Pole.
So I scoured the newspaper thinking where I might go.

Paris? I'd been there. And Cairo and Bali.
I'd flown over Boise, Hong Kong and New Delhi.
I imagined the globe. Spin it. Where would I pick?
I stopped in my tracks. And then it all clicked.

"I've got it!" I hollered.

"Let's load up the sleigh.

I'll need my red swimsuit and slippers. Away!

Also, some sunscreen and snacks for the ride,

a beach book, my swim fins, and traveler's guide.

I'm off to Hawai'i, the isles in the sea.

For the next few weeks I'll kick back and just be!"

We flew through the night, all my reindeers and I,
blazing past stars till something below caught my eye.
There, in the ocean, an incredible scene!
Hawai'i, lay floating, unreal as a dream.

"No time to dawdle," I called to my herd.
"Half an hour till sunrise. Fly swift as a bird!"
The reindeer bore down and we made it, post haste,
to the shores of Sunset Beach without a moment to waste.

HONOLULU NEWS
BIG WAVES!

December 5th

Hale'iwa—Big waves and monster swells brought out more than just beach goers and surfers at Pipeline today. Sightings of a white-haired man in a red suit were too numerous to count. Could it possibly be? Santa Claus is here in Hawai'i, right now?

We ran to the water and splashed in the blue,
saw seaweed and coral and fish by the slew!
I floated at peace in the water so clear
and said to the waves, "I think I belong here."

I **swam,** and I snorkeled. I hiked up Diamond Head.
I ate plate lunch and shave ice, "with snow cap," I said.
Learning how to hula and hang loose like a pro,
I baked in the sun saying, "Where I'm from there's snow!"

HONOLULU NEWS

December 10th

Waikīkī—It has been reported that a big room and an outdoor lānai suite for eight has been reserved at the Royal under the name S. Claus. Hoof marks have appeared in the sand, and the sounds of Christmas bells are in the air. Is it true that Santa has been spotted... on a surfboard? More details to come.

The North Pole,

oh it lingered and stuck in my mind.

And the longer I stayed, the bigger the bind.

Mrs. Claus called and asked, "When will you fly home?"

I heard nothing but surf and then put down the phone.

I was happy and tanned and relaxed as could be.

I was home, wasn't I, on this island in the sea?

SPECIAL 2 for 99¢

HONOLULU NEWS

December 15th

'Ewa Beach—A ruckus broke out in Aisle 2 at Longs this morning when a tanned, white-haired man, looking very much like Santa Claus bought up the remaining stock of chocolate-covered macadamia nuts, Saloon Pilot crackers, rubber slippers, and li hing mango saying, "This is too good not to share with the rest of the world." Minutes later, he was spotted in the line at Zippy's buying Zip Packs for nine…

See Ruckus, A8

We caught the Route 52 Bus and circled the Isle,
passed 'Ewa Beach and Wahiawā—it took us awhile!
We drove up to Hale'iwa, saw surfers galore,
and watched the winter swells crash up and down the North Shore.
At Kualoa Ranch we rode horses; we netted fish in Kahalu'u.
The plumerias smelled sweet as rain—there was so much to do!

The days passed too quickly.

Then the countdown began.

Just ten days till Christmas,

I needed to plan!

The North Pole was calling

for help in my shop.

But I was having fun in the sun.

I didn't want to see

another snowdrop.

HONOLULU NEW

December 20th

Honolulu, Hawai'i—This just in: Only days before Christmas and all letters addressed to S. Claus, North Pole, are being stamped "Return to Sender." There is no sign of Santa, at least not at the North Pole. But here in Hawai'i, it seems that there are many Santa sightings, taking us to Kailua Beach where Santa reportedly spent the day paddling canoe. If you are reading this, Santa, although we'd love for you to stay, the North Pole needs you!

SPORT

A mysterious letter arrived in the mail.

It read: *Santa Claus, General Delivery, Royal Hawaiian Hotel.*

Dear Santa,

We think it was you we saw swimming in the waves at Kailua Beach Park. (It's one of our faves.) But we have a few questions. We're a little concerned. Christmas is coming. Isn't it time you returned? We know it might be hard to leave, believe us, we know. And although you can't see yourself back in the snow, remember, you can take Hawai'i with you, if only in your heart. And why not teach the world about Hawai'i? We'll show you how to start. Meet us tomorrow. We'll help you get ready. There's lots to do. So we'll move fast and steady.

Love, Mehana and Kamuela

In Kailua town we met, my new friends and I.

Time was growing short, good thing we could fly!
We gathered seashells at Sandy's and beach glass at Tong's,
bought lei in Chinatown and beach buckets from Longs.
We grabbed turtles and dolphins from Ala Moana mall,
'ukulele and palaka shirts—large, medium, and small.
I memorized the sweet sounds of the slack-key guitar
in my Aloha shirt, my friends giggled, "So local, you are!"
We filled the big sleigh till we thought it would burst.
But before we went home, we made special stops first.

We flew Mehana and Kamuela to their hale by the sea,

and as we waved our goodbyes, they made me this plea:

"Don't forget us!" they yelled as the reindeer took flight.

"Remember what we taught you," they called to the night.

"With Hawaiʻi in your heart, wherever you go,

It will be like you're back here—in the Islands—we know!"

We made one last stop…

to the shores of Sunset Beach

where I first touched the land

I rested my sleigh and opened my hand.

I scooped up some sand, tucked it into my pouch,

gave the deer a great whistle, and for this I will vouch—

We took off in the air, and that sand made us *lighter*.

It lit up the sky, made the stars even brighter.

We made it home before
Christmas and Mrs. Claus jumped for joy.
"We knew you would make it, you jolly old boy!"
In our sleigh full of gifts, we flew into the night,
riding fast on the glow of the moon's winter light.
So this year, good children, don't be surprised
when you open your gifts and there on them lies
a layer of sand, or a necklace of shells,
or a conch that is roaring like big winter swells.
They are gifts from the islands, I'm sharing with you.
My way of turning a white Christmas into one that's bright blue.
A little Aloha, and the promise of more
Christmas days spent on a sandy seashore.

December 25

HONOLULU NEWS

December 25th

Honolulu, Hawai'i—It appears that children around the world have been waking up to something special—blue skies and stockings filled with sea shells and candy. There has been the smell of sunshine and—for a few minutes this morning—the whole world felt like it was waking up in Hawai'i.